Octavio

warms up

Written by Barbara Beak
Illustrated by Lynne Farmer

Child's Play (International) Ltd

Swindon   Bologna   New York

© M. Twinn 1991   ISBN 0-85953-786-2   Printed in Singapore

Octavia Octopus loved watching
the underwater ballet.

She liked dancing so much,
she dreamed of being a starfish.

So, one day, she decided
to take ballet lessons.

She ran, jumped, wriggled and writhed.
She rocked, rolled and twisted,
skipped, swung and swivelled.

She had so many legs,
she could dance four steps at the same time.

Until she got tied up in knots.

But when she arrived home,
she was stiff all over.

Her teacher, Madame Olga, explained,

"If you don't keep your joints warm,
you will get ballet ache.
You must have a scarf and leg-warmers."

Octavia's friends offered to lend theirs.
But they didn't have enough.

"You will have to knit your own," said Madame Olga.

"But I can't knit," wailed Octavia.

"Never mind, dear," said Madame Olga.
"I will show you. It is easy."

"First, we must gather plenty of stringy seaweed,
and we need some fishbones for needles."

Soon, Octavia was knitting
her very own leg-warmers.

She could knit four at a time!

Then, in no time at all,
she knitted her very own scarf.

From then on,
no matter how cold it was,
Octavia never suffered from ballet ache again.

All her friends asked her to knit
scarves and leg-warmers for them.

Octavia never became a starfish,
but her nifty fashion knitwear
won fame and fortune.

Octavia Octopus

Materials

Octavia's body: double knitting, jade green wool, approximately 25gms.

Octavia's scarf, headband, and eight leg-warmers:
mohair, fuchsia pink wool, approximately 15gms.

How to make Octavia Octopus

1. Cut a 1.5m length of yarn from the ball of green wool.

   Wind the remainder of the ball around a book measuring 28cm in height, working from top to bottom.

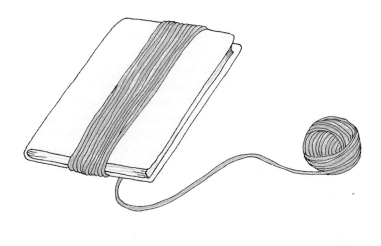

2. Cut a 20cm length of yarn from the 1.5m length.
Thread the 20cm strip between the book
and the wool at the top of the book, and tie a tight knot.

Cut through all the thicknesses of wool at the bottom of the book.

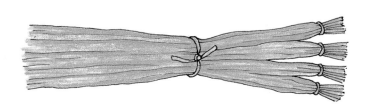

3. Lay the wool on a flat surface,
with the knot in the middle of the surface
and the two halves on either side.
Divide each half into four smaller bunches
(one for each leg), and use an elastic band
to keep each bunch separate from the other.

4. Bring all the legs together

5. Cut another 20cm length
   from your original length of yarn.
   Tie this around the legs,
   about 6cm down from the knot.
   The top part forms Octavia's head.

6. Cut the remainder of the length of yarn
   into eight pieces.

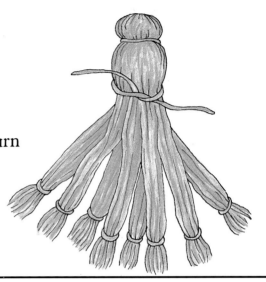

7. Plait each leg and tie tightly,
   about 3cm from the bottom,
   with each of the eight pieces of wool.

8. Embroider the eyes and mouth
   using the leftover yarn
   or embroidery thread.

Scarf

1. Using the pink wool, cast on four stitches.

2. Knit 39 rows.

3. Cast off.

4. Tie the scarf around Octavia's neck.

Leg-warmers (makes eight)

1. Using the pink wool, cast on 12 stitches.

   Knit five rows.

   Cast off.

   Sew the two longer edges together
   to form a tube.

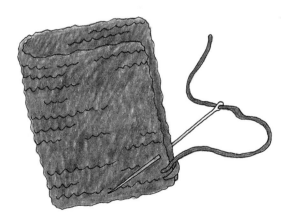

2. Altogether, make eight of these leg-warmers,
   and slip one onto each of Octavia's legs.

Headband

1. Using the pink wool, cast on two stitches.

2. Knit 47 rows.

3. Cast off.

4. Tie the headband around Octavia's head.